SPECIAL
VISITORS

Story by Jo Furtado
Pictures by Frédéric Joos

RED FOX

For Judy, and all her *very* special visitors

A Red Fox Book

Published by Random Century Children's Books
20 Vauxhall Bridge Road, London SW1V 2SA

A division of the Random Century Group
London Melbourne Sydney Auckland
Johannesburg and agencies throughout the world

First published by Andersen Press Ltd 1990

Red Fox edition 1992

Text © Jo Furtado 1990
Illustrations © Frederic Joos 1990

The right of Jo Furtado and Frederic Joos to be identified as the
author and illustrator of this work respectively has been
asserted by them in accordance with the Copyright, Designs and
Patents Act, 1988.

Printed in Hong Kong

ISBN 0 09 983470 7

Our house has lots and lots of special visitors. Here's the first of the day, coming right in through the window.

This special visitor doesn't come every day, but today he's brought oodles of letters – and a parcel! I wonder what's in it.

This special visitor *does* come every day, and *thinks* she
lives here. I wake up, then have my breakfast. She invites
herself to breakfast, then goes to sleep!

This special visitor shouldn't be here at all, my mum says!
He'll have to go. Just as well Topsy's not awake.

I've never seen this lady before. Mum – why are you
buying all these logs, Mum?

This is my friend, Jenny. Topsy's her cat. She likes
playing with my play-dough, and my bricks, and my
drum, and my teddy – and she likes drinking lemonade

and helping my mum to bake.

And that was Jenny's mum. And Topsy's mum.

If my mum turns around she'll see a special visitor she doesn't like. I do though. Her legs feel all tickly on the palm of my hand.

Here are two special visitors who both take away things
we don't want. She'll fly off while he's clattering and
bumping – but she'll be back soon.

Look – she's here again already.

Hooray! It's Tim and Aunty Linda. Come on, Tim. Let's play with my car again. Oh drat! That wasn't a very long visit. Please can't Tim stay a bit longer, please!

Well, I'm going outside to wave bye-bye. Bye-bye, Tim.
There's a bit of a wind out here. Better go inside, Mummy.

These must be the strangest special visitors we've had
today. Look, I think I'd better put them out. Bye-bye.

Oh! Mum... Mum! There's lots and lots of them all trying
to get in now! Help!

Grandma and Grandad – great! And Grandad's got a case.

What's in the case, Grandad? Pyjamas! Why? Oh – I know! Great! That means I can come into your bed for a cuddle in the morning.

You don't count, Dad. You're not a special visitor – you live here!

Go on, Dad! Do it again… again… again… again.

Who are these special visitors? Grandma says they came
to visit us this time last year too but I don't remember.
Isn't our house getting full?

And who's this? Oh – that's a nice song. I know this song. I think I'll join in. "The stars in the bright sky looked down where he lay, the little Lord Jesus asleep on the hay."

All those special visitors have made our house a happy place tonight, but I'm tired now. Goodnight, Mr Moon. I suppose you'll bc our last special visitor of the day...

Some bestselling Red Fox picture books